TAMING THE LAND

by
VeraLee Wiggins

YOUNG READER'S CHRISTIAN LIBRARY

Illustrations by
Tim Holtrop

A BARBOUR BOOK

ISBN 1-55748-774-X

Published by   Barbour and Company, Inc.
                  P.O. Box 719
                  Uhrichsville, OH 44683

95   96   97   98   99   5   4   3   2   1

TAMING
THE LAND

DAVID AND PA LOOKED FOR 160 ACRES TO CLAIM.

CHAPTER 1

David Moreland followed Pa across the dried prairie. Pa rode one of Jake's horses and David followed on Thunder, his big black gelding.

Jake—Jacob Case—was David's good friend. Actually, Jake wasn't very good. And he wasn't much of a friend, either.

David and his family had just arrived in Walla Walla Valley after traveling The Oregon Trail for five months. Because of a mean streak, Jake had treated David and nearly everyone else badly during the long journey.

This was the third day Pa and David had spent riding around looking for the perfect home, a place to make a donation claim. A donation claim was free land the government promised people for settling the new lands. David's family would get 160 acres, which

seemed like a whole world to him.

Suddenly, Pa pulled the slack from his horse's reins and held out his arm. David reined Thunder to a stop beside Pa.

Pa swept his arm around, indicating the prairie before them. "What do you think of this, son? Pretty a spot as I ever seen, with that little creek runnin' by."

He pointed at some rough, wood buildings to the west. "That's Fort Walla Walla over there. That's where the soldiers live. They keep the settlers safe from Indians." He grinned at David. "I like this place a lot. What do you think?"

David laughed out loud, just for the joy of living and the warm sunshine on his shoulders. Truly, this spot of ground didn't seem all that much different from any they'd been looking at, but it did look good. "I like it, Pa. Shall we get Mama and the girls to see how they like it?"

"PRETTY A SPOT AS I EVER SEEN. . . ."

Pa shook his head just as a huge rock hit Thunder on the back hip, toppling David to the ground. David landed on his side beside the big horse but jumped to his feet peering in the direction the rock had come from.

Just as he'd thought. Jake Case sat on his other horse twenty-five feet behind them, leaning back in his saddle and laughing as if he'd done something really funny.

Even though Jake was bigger than he, David felt like lobbing a rock right back at him. Not to hit the horse, but Jake. David loved animals. Jake had been abusing animals as well as people for as long as David had known him.

David prayed: *Keep reminding me I'm helping You do a good work in Jake, God. Make me treat him nice—no matter what.*

By this time, Thunder had regained his feet so David

A HUGE ROCK HIT THUNDER.

hopped onto his back, petting the powerful black neck. Unable to treat Jake decently at the moment, he moved to his father's side. "Ready to go back, Pa?" he asked, as if nothing had happened. "We might as well go get our donation claim."

Pa edged his horse a bit closer to David's and dropped his arm around David's shoulders. "I could stay here and look at it forever, son, but let's go make it ours." David silently thanked God for helping him not return Jake's meanness. He silently thanked Pa, too, for ignoring Jake.

When they reached the covered wagons, Mama, and his two sisters, Annie, 18, and Katie, 13, rushed to meet them. "Did you find our place?" Katie asked. Her blue eyes danced, and her dark blond hair ruffled in the breeze.

A big smile nearly covered Pa's face. "We sure did, kitten. You'll love it."

DAVID THANKED GOD FOR HELPING HIM.

"Does it have trees?" Annie asked.

David laughed out loud. "How many trees do you see around here? Not a tree on the place, Annie, but we can get some from the riverbank."

In a little while, the whole family trooped into the third building on the north side of The Street. The Street was a Nez Perce Indian trail with four rickety buildings on each side. The name on this building said Baldwin Brothers, Licensed Traders. Someone had told them the donation land claim office was in the back.

As David walked through the rough wood building, he saw daylight between nearly every board.

Less than a half-hour later, the family rushed back outside. The long paper Pa held in his hands said that if they lived on the land and farmed it for a few years, they would own the land free and clear.

"Let's go build our new house," Katie said.

"LET'S GO BUILD OUR NEW HOUSE!"

Pa laughed and hugged his plump, little daughter. "It's not quite that simple, Katie. We have to go up in the Blue Mountains to get the logs. But we can move the wagons over there so people will know it's taken."

By evening, the wagons sat side by side about twenty feet from the gurgling creek. Pa turned the oxen loose to graze, but David tied Thunder. He wouldn't chance anyone taking his special horse.

After they ate a supper of beans, side meat, and biscuits, Pa called David. "I need your help, son," he said with a merry twinkle. "Remember the last thing we did before starting on The Trail?"

David thought hard, remembering back. "Ate in a restaurant?"

Pa laughed again. "No, son. We did it to the wagon. In the floor."

Finally, David remembered. They'd hid money under the floorboards! He'd forgotten all about it. "Yes!

"I NEED YOUR HELP, SON."

We put it under the floorboards."

Pa pulled a screwdriver from his pocket. "Let's get that money, son, so we can have something else to eat tomorrow."

Pa undid the screws while David lifted the boards. Pa pulled out the bag and handed it to David. "Wanta count it?" he asked. "There's enough there to build our cabin and to live on until we get our farm going."

David handed it back. "That's a lot of money. You'd better keep it, Pa."

That night, Mark Mathis, Annie's friend, joined the family for worship around a small camp fire. Then, David took his blanket and wrapped up in it on the ground. Pa and Ma slept in one wagon and Annie and Katie used the other. David had slept on the ground ever since they'd left Missouri.

"Thank You for giving me such a good day, Father," he said looking up at the starry skies. "And for-

"WANTA COUNT IT?"

give Jake. You and I'll get him tamed yet, won't we? Good night, God. I love you."

"Who says anyone's gonna tame me?" a snarling voice asked. Jake dropped his blanket on the ground beside David's and flopped into it. He'd slept beside David every night on The Trail. Jake's mother had died two years earlier, so Jake only had his father, and he didn't pay much attention to him.

David hadn't expected to see much of Jake now that they'd arrived. "I thought you wanted to be God's friend after He saved you from drowning," he said.

"Sometimes I do," Jake said, "but sometimes I like to have fun. Weren't that a good trick I played on you today?"

David jerked upright in his blanket. "You mean hitting Thunder with a rock? That wasn't funny at all. Don't you know you hurt him?"

"I din't hear him cryin'."

"WHO SAYS ANYONE'S GONNA TAME ME?"

David couldn't handle any more of Jake, so he turned over and closed his eyes.

"Come on, Davy! Get up! We have lots to do today."

David pulled the blanket tighter around his shoulders when Pa called. He glanced at the spot beside him and saw only the mashed grass. Jake had gone back to where he had come from. David looked up at Pa and laughed out loud. They were here in the Walla Walla Valley, ready to start their new life.

After breakfast, Pa invited David to go into the Blues to look for logs.

"I'm going too," Katie said, her plump body shaking with eagerness.

"No, you aren't," Pa said. "You go to the store with Mama to buy some good food. If we bring a heavy load of logs, Davy and I'll have to walk all the way back and it's a long way."

JAKE HAD GONE BACK TO WHERE HE HAD COME FROM.

David helped Pa remove the wagon's bonnet and all the wood they could get off to make it lighter for the oxen to pull. Then following the well-tromped trail, they found themselves at a sawmill in three hours. Rough boards lay everywhere in neat stacks. Big piles of small logs lay beyond the boards.

A bearded man appeared almost as soon as they'd jumped down from the wagon. "Reckon y'all lookin' to build a cabin?"

Pa nodded. "Looks like we came to the right place. Whadda we need?"

"Well, ya gonna use boards or logs?"

"I was thinkin' on logs. That'd be cheaper, wouldn't it?" After talking with the man awhile, they piled a load of logs onto the wagon.

"Looks as how we'll have to walk," Pa said as the oxen struggled with the oversized load.

David didn't mind. In fact, he'd rather walk, with

"RECKON Y' ALL LOOKIN' TO BUILD A CABIN?"

the sun shining on his shoulders. "Here, let me guide the oxen." Leading the oxen, he grinned at a thought that popped into his mind. "We ought to take our donation claim up here, Pa, among the trees. Annie'd like that." David watched eagerly for Pa's answer.

Pa smiled. "They don't let people take claims up here, son. Guess they want to get the land settled in an orderly way. 'Twould be a long way from anyone else, too. Maybe dangerous."

At almost the instant Pa said dangerous, one of the oxen stumbled on a small log lying at the edge the trail. The load of logs began shuddering, then shaking hard.

David jumped out of the way, but his heart almost stopped when Pa moved toward the wagon. He shoved his shoulder against it hard. "Get out of there, Pa," David screamed. "You can't hold it!"

A moment later the load shifted and dumped!

"GET OUT OF THERE, PA. YOU CAN'T HOLD IT!"

THOSE LOGS HURT PA BAD!

CHAPTER 2

"Pa!" David screamed. "Run!" Pa ran, but the logs seemed to be chasing him. He almost outran them, but two bounced off two others and hit him hard in the back. Pa threw out his arms to break the fall, but the logs landed on him, smashing him to the ground. Those logs hurt Pa bad!

"Help, God!" David cried loudly.

Not a sound broke the silence of the woods. David grabbed the top log and moved it a little, but he couldn't do it alone without hurting Pa more.

David bowed his head and spoke quietly this time. "Father, thank You for loving us so much. And for caring about everything that happens to us. Pa's hurt, and I'm not strong enough to get the logs off. Send someone to help, Father God. Please. I never needed You so much as I do now. I ask in Jesus' name. Amen."

David opened his eyes to see a lone rider coming up the trail toward the mill. Unable to restrain himself, he raced toward the man, thanking God as he ran. "You're the answer to my prayer, sir," he called as they approached each other. "Hurry! My pa's hurt."

The man nudged his pretty chestnut mare into a trot. David soon saw a grin cross his face. "An answer to prayer am I?" he repeated. "Well, I wondered why Faith and I came up here. Where's your pa?"

David pointed and started running back. The horse and man followed.

Soon, they found Pa with the two logs crosswise over him. "Think you can get these things off me?" he grunted. "I'm plumb mashed."

The man moved to the log David couldn't lift. "Now, we'll have to take it real easy here, son. Let's see if we can get this off without moving the other one. Grab hold. And be careful." The man looked up

"YOU'RE THE ANSWER TO MY PRAYER, SIR!"

into the bright blue sky. "You've brought us this far, Father. Help us to move these logs without hurting him. Thank You, Lord."

The two worked carefully together and soon the bigger log lay beside the trail. "That thing was heavy," David said. "I gotta rest a minute."

The big man chuckled. "Our Mighty Lord gave us the strength to do the job though, didn't He? Grab this next one. He'll help us again."

The other log lay beside the trail in ten minutes. As they laid the log down, Pa moaned. "We've hurt him," David whispered looking down at Pa. He'd never seen Pa so still.

Blood oozed from his face and head. His arms looked strange, but they weren't bleeding.

"I think he's all right, son." The stranger peered into David's eyes. "What's your name?"

"David Moreland."

"LORD, HELP US TO MOVE THESE LOGS...."

"I'm Paul Reynolds." the kind stranger said. He looked toward the blue sky again. "Thank You for the strength and steady hands, Lord. We coulda never done it without You." He motioned to a log ten feet off the trail. "You sit down over there, Dave, while I see what's up with your pa."

David felt more than glad to sit down. In fact, his legs felt wobbly. He watched as Mr. Reynolds went over Pa's body inch by inch. Finally, the man's kind eyes met David's. "He's mostly just banged up, Dave. His face and head are scraped purty good, and his arms are broken. But he'll heal up."

A huge relief poured through David's body. Then he remembered where they were—logs all over, and Pa unconscious on the ground.

He jumped up and knelt beside his father. "Pa. Pa!" he said urgently. "Wake up, Pa. You're hurt."

Pa's eyelids flickered, then opened. His eyes looked

"I'M PAUL REYNOLDS."

blank for a moment then settled on David's face. "Somethin's—hurtin'—me," he mumbled.

Mr. Reynolds joined David on his knees beside Pa. "I'm Paul Reynolds, Mr. Moreland. A couple of your logs jumped you. But you're all right—just skinned up a little and two broken arms. You just take it easy while we get you home."

Pa's pinched face relaxed; he gave a slight nod and closed his eyes.

Mr. Reynolds got to his feet. "Help me find four straight little trees, David. If we don't splint your pa's arms before we move him, your ma'll hear him yelling from here." David gladly joined the search and before long, four strong saplings lay on the trail beside Pa. The man God sent to help cut each tree to the right length. "Can you hold him while I set his arms?" Mr. Reynolds asked. "I'll just pull gently until they snap into place."

THE MAN GOD SENT CUT EACH TREE TO THE RIGHT LENGTH.

David held Pa tight while Mr. Reynolds pulled. He gritted his teeth and tried not to hear Pa moaning, and Mr. Reynolds grunting as he strained. When the first arm snapped into place, David felt like shouting for joy.

"We aren't through yet, Dave." Mr. Reynolds said, pulling off his shirt. "Give me your shirt, too." Then he tore them both into long strips. After wrapping the set arm in lots of cloth, he tied two of the saplings tight against the arm.

When they repeated the procedure for the other arm, Pa let out a few small groans. Mostly, he kept his pain to himself.

"You're a brave man, Mr. Moreland," Mr. Reynolds said when he finished. "I know I hurt you some—in fact, a whole lot."

David scrambled to his feet. "Are we going to leave the logs? We paid lots of money for them."

"YOU'RE A BRAVE MAN, MR. MORELAND. . . ."

"Your pa's gotta ride in the wagon, Dave. I'll tell you what. You run back to the mill and get a paper sayin' these logs belong to the Morelands. While you're gone, I'll get your pa ready to go."

When David returned, he stuck the paper onto a limb stub on one of the logs. Mr. Reynolds finished preparing Pa for the trip home. *Thank You, Lord,* David said silently. *I'd have been happy to see anyone coming down the trail, but I can tell he's a really good man. When I asked, You sent the best.*

Going down the hill was easier on the oxen than going up, and they had to stop for Pa only a few times. They arrived home by late afternoon. After explaining to Mama what had happened, Mr. Reynolds offered to take Pa to Fort Walla Walla. "I'm one of their medics," he explained, "and we take in people when they need us. Your husband will take lots of care during the next few weeks." He chuckled. "Someone will

"YOUR HUSBAND WILL TAKE LOTS OF CARE...."

even have to feed him."

Mama said she'd be glad to care for Pa. He wanted to stay with his family, so they put him into his and Ma's feather bed on the ground. Mama invited Mr. Reynolds to stay for supper, but he had to get back to Fort Walla Walla to his duties.

David had to tell Ma and the girls what had happened several times to satisfy them. "Aw, it wasn't that bad," Pa finally said. "You 'n that young man you got did just fine." Then into the silence he added, "Wonder who's gonna build our cabin?"

Mama led in their Bible reading and prayer that night. They all thanked God for sending Dr. Reynolds to help them.

David put his blanket near Pa and Ma so he could help if Pa needed anything.

He hadn't fallen asleep yet when Jake dropped his blanket beside David's. Then Jake noticed Pa. "Who's that?" he grunted.

MAMA LED IN THEIR BIBLE READING AND PRAYER.

"It's Pa," David said. "He got hurt today and can't climb into the wagon."

Jake got up, moved his blanket about ten feet away and crawled back in.

David wondered why he had done that but didn't worry about it. "Thank You for answering my prayer today, God," he whispered into the quiet darkness. "I can hardly believe You sent a real doctor. And you must have sent him even before I prayed. But You knew what would happen and that I would pray, didn't You? Somewhere the Bible says You'll answer before we pray."

The next morning, the shaggy-haired doctor from Fort Walla Walla came to check on Pa. "Doin' just great, Mr. Moreland," he said. "Thanks to the good Lord."

"Thanks to you, too, Dr. Reynolds," David said.

The man shook his head. "Don't ever give credit to a man, son. A man can't do anything. But with God

"DOIN' JUST GREAT. . .THANKS TO THE GOOD LORD."

we can do everything." He grinned at David. "And call me Paul. I'm only twenty-three."

David had a question for Dr. Reyn—Paul. "How come you rode up that trail to the mill yesterday? Were you looking for logs or boards?"

The man grinned and shook his light brown head. "I sure wasn't, Dave. Things got kind of caught up at The Fort, so I got some free time. I decided to take a ride and that's where I ended up. Way I figure it, God nudged me right up that trail."

Jake wandered by a little later. "Wanna go get the logs?" he asked David. "We'll get 'em, then you 'n me can build the cabin."

David's stomach flipped. He could see Jake purposely dumping the logs just for fun. "I don't think so, Jake. No telling what you'd do to the logs or the oxen or even me."

"WAY I FIGURE IT, GOD NUDGED ME RIGHT UP THAT TRAIL."

THE BOYS. . .HEADED TOWARD THE BLUES.

CHAPTER 3

"Aw, I won't do nothin'. Let's go."

Pa, who sat on a box by the campfire, pale but alert, spoke up. "Why don't you go, Dave? Someone up there'll help you get them on the wagon. It would be a big help."

So the boys yoked the oxen and headed toward the Blues. "You really asked your God to send someone yesterday when yer pa got hurt?" Jake asked as they walked beside the oxen in the warm sunshine.

David didn't mind relating the incident again. Maybe something would sink into Jake's thick skull sometime. "Yes. Then, I opened my eyes to see Paul riding toward me. I'd have been happy for just any-one, Jake. But God sent a doctor from The Fort. Isn't He great?"

Jake gazed off toward the mountains. Then his face

snapped toward David. A lazy grin appeared as he nodded. "Yeah. I guess He is."

David wanted to shout for joy but contented himself with one high jump into the air.

The boys finally reached the spilled logs. A big man came from the mill to help them load the logs onto the wagon. They had to rest several times. During one of their rests, all three shared the good lunch Mama had packed. David carefully guided the oxen this time, so they wouldn't have another mishap.

They arrived at the campsite just before dark. Both boys as well as the oxen were ready for a good night's sleep.

The next day, Pa seemed pretty chipper—for a man who couldn't use either arm. It looked strange to see Mama feeding Pa, but David knew it had to be. After breakfast, Pa sent Jake and David back for another load of logs, saying he'd already paid for it. The boys

A BIG MAN FROM THE MILL CAME TO HELP THEM. . . .

went twice more before Pa thought they had enough.

Pa told the boys they'd have to wait until Mark Mathis, Annie's friend, or Paul Reynolds could come help them get started on the cabin.

One day, Jake came into camp full of excitement. "Remember that last river we crossed gittin' here? I just heard there's lots of fish in it. Let's go get some."

The boys jumped on their horses and rode south. Soon, a row of trees appeared in the distance. When they reached the trees, they found the pretty little river flowing past. Several boys and a few girls sat on the bank with poles in their hands. A ways farther west, three Indian boys fished. They didn't use poles but held the fishing lines in their hands.

"Ketchin' somethin'?" Jake asked some of the white boys.

One tall, skinny boy pointed into his basket. "Lookit them beauties." David counted six fish, maybe trout,

"KETCHIN' SOMETHIN'?"

from about ten inches to a foot and a half.

He and Jake hurried to a vacant spot and, after threading long fishing worms on their hooks, dropped them into the water.

Neither got a bite, and after awhile, David grew sleepy. He leaned back on the bank of the river and dozed a little. When he awakened, Jake, his horse, and his pole were gone.

He could have woke me up, David thought. He'd have gone back with Jake. The other white people had gone, too, but David stayed awhile. Just as the sun started to set, one of the Indian boys approached him. He looked friendly, so David felt only a little fear. The boy signaled for David to follow him. Then, he showed David a whole basket of fish, and motioned for David to take some.

David took three of the smaller ones and looked at the Indian boy wondering how to thank him. The boy

HE LOOKED FRIENDLY. . . .

offered David some more, then held out his hand at
several different heights from the ground. David un-
derstood! He wondered if there were other kids in his
family. David showed with his hands about how tall
each person in his family was, then held up a finger
for each member and added one more for Jake. He
had six fingers up. The Indian grinned and gave him
three more fish, nice big ones. David thanked him the
best he could, mounted Thunder, and let the big horse
gallop back to the campsite. As he and Thunder sped
back to camp, David felt light and happy. Maybe he
could be friends with the Indians.

Mama proudly fried the fish, and about the time
she took them from the skillet, Jake showed up.

"Who gave you them fish?" he asked.

"One of the Indians," David said. "They had a lot
and everyone else had gone."

Jake sneered. "No he din't. You stole 'em. That's

THE INDIAN GRINNED AND GAVE HIM THREE MORE FISH.

what you did." Everyone enjoyed the treat anyway.

That night when Jake dropped his blanket beside him, David decided to try one more time with Jake. He sat up and faced Jake. "Do you believe I love God, Jake?" he asked.

"I guess you do."

"Well, God gave people ten rules to follow, and one of them says we can't steal. Know why, Jake? God's book says we should treat others the way we want them to treat us. I wouldn't want anyone to steal the fish I caught. Would you?"

"I'd clean 'em good. Nobody better never steal nothin' from me, Davy baby."

David chuckled out loud. "Well, there you are, Jake. I don't want anyone to steal from me, so I don't steal from them. Believe me?"

Jake didn't answer for so long David thought he must have fallen asleep—or he didn't believe.

"DO YOU BELIEVE I LOVE GOD, JAKE?"

"Naw, you wouldn't steal from no one. Not even a savage redskin. Good night, Davy baby."

The next morning, Paul Reynolds, the Fort Walla Walla doctor, came to check on Pa. After deciding Pa was doing well, he turned his eyes upward. "Thanks for being so faithful, Lord. We can always count on You." Then he turned to David. "When are we starting your cabin?"

David felt proud to have Paul treating him as an adult. "I'm ready, but I don't know exactly how."

"Well," Paul said, "let's get going then. Where's that other boy I saw you with?"

"That's Jacob Case. He's around somewhere."

"No matter. We'll get going on it. He'll probably show up and help."

Paul and David dragged some of the largest logs to a low hill. Then, they put them into small ditches they'd dug, one on each side of the cabin. "Now we'll

"WHEN ARE WE STARTING YOUR CABIN?"

saw notches out of them and place logs the other way."

Katie and Annie brought David and Paul cold drinks twice during the day.

By the end of the day, all the outside walls stood three logs high.

David had never in his life gone to bed feeling so proud of himself.

Jake nearly fell over the walls when he came to sleep beside David. "Watcha doin', tryna kill me?" he grunted flopping to the ground.

BY THE END OF THE DAY, ALL THE OUTSIDE WALLS
STOOD THREE LOGS HIGH.

JAKE STUCK AROUND. . .AND WORKED HARD ALL DAY.

CHAPTER 4

"No, you fell over the cabin," David whispered. "We started building it today. Isn't it great?"

"No, it ain't. Thought I was gonna help."

"We just got started. Where were you all day? Helping your pa build your cabin?"

"Naw. Pa's happy in the tent. Guess he figgers it won't get cold." He pulled his blanket around his neck. "Seems to me, it's purty cold already."

David used two blankets now, so Jake sure enough could be cold. Maybe he could find another one for Jake tomorrow. "Come and help tomorrow, Jake. We need you real bad."

Jake stuck around for breakfast the next morning and worked hard all day. He still stayed after supper. And for the family's worship time.

After worship Pa thanked Jake for helping. "If you

help all the way, I'll give you a small nugget. Know what that is? It's a hunk of gold worth $50. People use them for money out here."

"I don't need no nugget," Jake muttered.

After Pa talked to Jake, David followed Mama to the wagon and asked for a blanket for Jake. She gladly gave it to him.

When David gave Jake the blanket, he grabbed it eagerly and spun himself into it. But he didn't say a word. Not even "Thank you."

The next morning, Pa asked David and Jake to go to Fort Walla Walla and buy them a milk cow.

"Kin I have some milk when you git the cow?" Jake asked as they approached the rough wooden door of the big building.

"Sure. You can have all you want." Then a man in uniform opened the door.

Jake stepped in front of David. "We need a milk

JAKE EAGERLY SPUN HIMSELF INTO THE BLANKET.

cow," he said. "One that gives a lot of milk."

The man shook his head. "Sorry, boys. We don't have a milking cow on the place. Won't for a couple of months. Ain't none in the valley right now."

Jake seemed even more disappointed than David felt.

He worked alongside David and Paul all day every day. They chopped notches in the logs and stacked others across the notches. Nearly every day Jake had an "accident" which he thought hilariously funny. One day, he jerked a log out of Paul's hands, and it dropped—right on Paul's foot.

Another day as he took a drink, he dropped the entire dipper of water—all over Pa who sat on a log watching.

Yet another time while he and David carried a log, he gave it a shove, knocking David down. The log dropped on David.

"SORRY, BOYS. WE DON'T HAVE A MILKING COW. . . ."

David stayed in close contact with God, constantly praying to treat Jake better than he deserved. He hoped if no one paid any attention, Jake would get tired of his tricks.

Pa scolded Jake sometimes, from his log seat, but Jake just grinned.

One day, Annie's friend, Mark, came to help. Jake saw him approaching on his sorrel mare. "I'm gettin' outta here," he said, taking off.

When Pa got better, he stood with the boys showing them what to do, though the splints still held his arms tight to his sides.

They made the walls higher than a man's head, leaving openings for windows and two doors. Mama and the girls chinked between the logs with mud to keep out the cold. When the outside walls were all finished, they put a floor inside made from half logs, the flat side up.

THEY MADE THE WALLS HIGHER THAN A MAN'S HEAD.

Then Jake and David made another trip to the mill to buy rough boards. They used these to divide the cabin into the main room—the kitchen where they'd spend all their time—and two small bedrooms. They put in a floor above the kitchen part which formed a loft, with a ladder on the wall. This would be David's bedroom.

No one in the little town of Steptoeville in Walla Walla Valley in Washington Territory had glass, so they settled for some soft material called isinglass for the windows. It allowed light into the house, but they couldn't see out.

The same evening they finished the cabin, the Morelands moved their clothes and food into it. They didn't have any furniture, so the move didn't take long. Jake helped.

"We'd best bring in the alfalfa seed," Pa said. They'd brought several barrels of the new kind of hay

ROUGH BOARDS DIVIDED THE CABIN INTO THREE ROOMS.

seed from Missouri. "If that got ruined, we couldn't replace it. I'm countin' on that to make us a good livin'."

"Why don't you sleep in the loft with me?" David asked Jake after they carried in the seed. "It's getting too cold outside."

Jake gladly brought his two blankets in and climbed the ladder with David after the family, sitting on the floor, thanked God for their house and read some Bible chapters.

David squirmed in his blankets, thinking how much harder the boards were than the ground.

"Hey, Davy baby, ain't this a lot warmer than sleepin' outside?"

David asked God to forgive him for complaining, even to himself.

The next morning, Pa sent David and Jake to The Street to see if anyone in the area made furniture. "I

"WHY DON'T YOU SLEEP IN THE LOFT WITH ME?"

don't care if it's rough," Pa said. "We need a table and somethin' to sit on right bad. A sideboard for our food'd be a big help, too." As they turned their horses toward the shacky business buildings, David noticed a covered wagon sitting there. As they rode past it, a middle-sized gray, black, and white dog came running toward them, its tail wagging. Not barking, it just seemed eager to meet them.

Jake followed David into the general store, the first building on the south side of The Street.

"'Fraid no one's had time to start makin' furniture yet," the owner explained in answer to David's question. "Can't your Pa make somethin' just fer now?"

David explained about Pa's broken arms.

They tried all the seven other buildings, too, four on each side of The Street spreading over about a block.

When they reached the end of the buildings, they

DAVID EXPLAINED ABOUT PA'S BROKEN ARMS.

found a creek blocking the end of The Street. "Wanta go wading?" David asked, wondering if the fall weather might be too cold for playing in the water.

"What ya take me for, a little kid?" Jake growled.

"Okay, let's go back," David said. "Maybe I can make some furniture for Pa."

"You go on," Jake said as David mounted Thunder. "I got somethin' else to do now."

David took it easy and let Thunder wander around some going back. Just before they reached the log cabin, Jake galloped past on his Indian horse. David touched Thunder's sides with his shoes. "Come on, boy," he whispered, "we can't let him beat us on that little thing." Thunder took off, overtaking Jake in a few minutes. "What're you running from?" David asked laughing.

Jake looked shocked at David's remark. "What's it to you, Moreland? Whattaya think you are, my

"WHAT'RE YOU RUNNING FROM?"

mother?"

Giving his pony a fierce kick in the sides, he turned the animal south, and left David wondering what had happened.

As David rode on toward his place, he suddenly remembered seeing something in Jake's hand. Was that what had gotten him so upset?

Pa showed disappointment that the boys hadn't found someone to build furniture. Mama took it better. "Don't worry about it, Pa," she said. "We've been livin' out of barrels 'n boxes for six months. I reckon we can keep on awhile."

When Ma called them for dinner, Jake hadn't returned—for the first time since they'd started building the cabin.

About mid-afternoon a tall, bearded man rode up to the cabin, asking to talk to Pa. David remembered him from the general store. Maybe they'd found some-

A TALL, BEARDED MAN RODE UP TO THE CABIN.

one to make furniture. "I'm Lew McMorris," he said reaching a hand to Pa.

Pa grinned. "Sorry, McMorris. Right now I don't shake with anyone."

McMorris looked embarrassed when he saw Pa's useless arms. "Sorry about your accident," he said. "Hate to bother you at a time like this but yer better off knowin'. One of yer boys just took a nugget from my cash box."

"ONE OF YER BOYS JUST TOOK A NUGGET FROM MY CASH BOX."

"I NEED THAT FIFTY DOLLARS, MORELAND."

CHAPTER 5

McMorris looked embarrassed when he accused Moreland's boy of taking a gold nugget. "I need that fifty dollars, Moreland. But even more, yer boy needs to learn that ain't the way to get money."

Pa gave David a quick glance. "This here's my son. Know what the man's talking about, Davy?"

David shook his head, wondering if maybe he knew more about it than he wanted to. "I was in your store a while ago, Mr. McMorris, but I didn't take anything. I didn't even know you had a nugget."

McMorris wore a worried look. "I remember this'n, but he ain't the one. It's the other boy."

Pa's face suddenly showed understanding. "Where's Jake, Davy?" he asked quietly.

"I don't know, Pa. He didn't come back with me."

McMorris took a step toward David. "I don't like

to be hard, son, but that nugget represents a week's work, and I've got to have it. You'd better go get your brother right now."

"Right now, Jake's at his pa's tent," Pa said. "But he spends tolerable bit o' time here. Ain't got a fit home. No ma, and from what I figger, not much of a pa. But we'll find him and see what's up. Sorry, McMorris. That's the best we can do."

"That's fine, Moreland," McMorris said reaching a hand toward Pa again and instantly dropping it. "Sorry, fergot about your arms. I know you'll be doin' all you can. I'd best be gettin' back to the store now. Might be your boy shouldn't be spendin' all his time with that other'n."

When the man left, Pa turned to David. "You got anything more to tell me now?"

David didn't know much more than he'd told, but he couldn't lie to Pa. "Not much. Jake rode past

"YOU GOT ANYTHING MORE TO TELL ME NOW?"

Thunder and me, so we caught him. He got mad and took off when I asked what he was doing. I'm afraid he did it, Pa."

Jake didn't return until the next day about noon.

Mama welcomed him eagerly. "Come and help us eat this pot of beans," she said dishing up the food.

David watched to see what Pa would do. He didn't say anything to Jake until after the meal ended. Then he called Jake to him and calmly and kindly told him about McMorris's visit. "Do you still have the nugget?" he asked.

Jake shook his head. "I gave it to my pa. Thought he might need it."

Pa leaned forward to hear Jake better. "Did he ask where you got it?"

"Naw. He don't care nuthin' about me. Didn't even thank me fer it. Didn't even act like I was there after I gave it to him."

"I GAVE THE NUGGET TO MY PA."

David thought about Jake not thanking him for the blanket and other things. Maybe Jake couldn't help being like his pa.

"I'm sorry, Jake," Pa said softly. "I wish things were better for you. Remember, I said I'd give you a nugget when we finished buildin'? Well, I reckon the house is about done, so I'll give it to you now. Would you take it to McMorris? The man needs it right bad."

Jake took the nugget, climbed onto his horse, and started off toward The Street. David started to follow on Thunder. "Whatcha think yer doin', Davy baby? Checkin' to see if I run off with it?"

David turned Thunder south and touched his sides with his shoes. Thunder rolled into a gallop, and they had a long fast ride together.

"What did McMorris say when he got his nugget back?" Pa asked as David slid down Thunder's round side.

THUNDER ROLLED INTO A GALLOP....

David shook his head. "Jake didn't want me to go, so I didn't."

Pa didn't say any more but David could tell he was worried. "Want me to ask McMorris, Pa?"

Pa shook his head. "You might run into Jake. He needs to think we trust him. Love him, too. He stole that nugget to get his pa to notice him, you know."

When Jake returned two days later, Pa treated him like a son, and didn't even ask about the nugget.

When David and Jake settled down in the loft that night, Jake wrapped up in his two blankets and turned to David. "Your pa's purty good," he said. "He trusted me to take that nugget back, din't he?"

"Yeah," David said, "he knew you would."

Jake fidgeted another moment. "McMorris ain't too bad neither. He din't yell at me er nothin'. He sort of acted like I done something good for him. Gave me two pieces of candy." He held out a hand to David.

PA TREATED JAKE LIKE A SON.

"Here's yours. I saved it for you."

"Thanks, Jake." David took the piece of peppermint, laid it on the floor beside his blanket, and fell asleep.

One day David and Jake heard that some church held services in Galbraith's Saloon and told Pa about it. "My family ain't going into a saloon for any reason," he said. "We'll just keep right on having our church here. That's not so bad, is it?"

The next day, Mama sent David to the store for soap. Jake piled onto his horse and rode along. McMorris acted as if Jake and David were his two favorite customers. Even gave them extra soap.

When the boys left the store, David heard a dog making an awful racket. "Let's see what's up!" he said running toward the uproar.

As they rounded the building, they found the black, gray, and white dog lunging at a small animal it had

"LET'S SEE WHAT'S UP!"

crowded against a building. "Get away!" David yelled. The dog kept lunging and barking.

"Let's grab the dog, Jake!" David yelled. Just as he threw himself onto the dog the little black animal with a white stripe turned its back, and David felt sicker than he ever had in his life. As he vomited on the ground, he heard Jake yelling.

"Hoo, Davy baby, I'm goin' home. Don't never come near me again."

David heard Jake roaring with laughter, then silence. David's eyes burned so badly, he couldn't see anything. After he stopped throwing up, he sat down in the dust. He stayed there for a long, long time until he could see out of his watering eyes.

The first thing he saw was the dog rolling around in the dust, then sliding on its back, and finally trying to bury its head in the dirt. David chuckled out loud. He might be the only person in the entire world who

DAVID FELT SICKER THAN HE EVER HAD IN HIS LIFE.

knew exactly how that dog felt. After a while longer, he decided he'd better get Thunder and go home. But when he went after Thunder, the big horse had disappeared.

He opened the door to the general store to ask if McMorris knew anything about his horse.

"Get out of here and shut that door!" McMorris yelled. "Go roll in the creek!"

David shut the door, realizing how horrible he must smell. He might as well walk home. Probably, they wouldn't even want him there.

He walked home thinking about Thunder. He couldn't bear even thinking about living without his horse. "Help him to be all right, God," he prayed over and over.

It seemed to take forever to walk the two miles home, but finally, he approached the cabin.

"Run, everyone," Jake's guttural voice yelled.

THE WALK HOME SEEMED TO TAKE FOREVER.

"Don't let Davy baby get near ya."

Pa hurried toward David. "Sorry, son," he called. "You better go soak in the creek awhile." He pointed north and west. "Go down that way and take off your clothes. Maybe you'll get rid of most of the smell."

David did as Pa said, but the brisk November day didn't make the cold water feel all that good. After awhile, Pa came with a bar of soap. "Better use that all up," he said tossing it to David. "Mama's got some hot soup for you when you get through."

After another little while, Pa brought a folded blanket and laid it on the dried grass. "Wrap up in that when you're through. Leave your clothes for now."

He went back to the house leaving David alone. David's teeth chattered so much he could hardly scrub with the soap. He couldn't smell the horrible stink anymore, but his stomach still felt upset. He climbed out of the water, managed to get the blanket around

"YOU BETTER GO SOAK IN THE CREEK AWHILE," PA SAID.

him, and staggered to the cabin. Shaking so hard from the cold made it hard to keep his legs under him.

Jake ran out the cabin door just before David reached it. "You ain't comin' in here!" he yelled.

Then Annie came out with two more blankets. She stopped twenty feet from David and laid the blankets on the ground. Then she backed up really fast. "Put these around you," she yelled. "Mama will bring you some bread and soup. That'll help you get warm."

David felt a black cloud descend on him. "Can't I have some dry clothes? And aren't you going to let me in?"

"AREN'T YOU GOING TO LET ME IN?"

"IF YOU'D GOT ON THUNDER, YOUR PA WOULD'VE HAD
TO SHOOT HIM."

CHAPTER 6

Annie shook her head sadly when David asked if he could come into the cabin. "We'd all have to go outside then. Sorry, Davy."

Jake came out and stood a distance away. "Din't you forget somethin' when you came home, Davy baby?"

David couldn't even think about Jake's meanness right then. "No, I didn't. You're the one who forgot something. Me."

Jake laughed as if that were the funniest thing he'd ever heard. "What about Thunder, Davy baby?"

Thunder! He'd forgotten Thunder. "Somebody took Thunder, Jake. Do you know where he is?"

Jake pointed off behind the cabin where Thunder grazed happily. "If you'd got on Thunder, your pa would've had to shoot him." He laughed again.

David felt furious at Jake for taking Thunder. Yet if he'd ridden Thunder smelling as he did, the poor horse would be in trouble, too. Not shot, but maybe sick.

He stomped off where he wouldn't have to think about Jake for awhile.

That night the whole family joined David outside for their Bible reading and prayer. After they'd finished, even before they went inside, David began to feel lonely. "Will you sleep out here with me, Jake?" he asked, knowing Jake wouldn't.

Jake laughed out loud. "I din't tangle with that there skunk, Davy baby. Can you think of any good reason why I'd sleep out here in the cold?" With that he disappeared into the cabin.

Just what David had expected. He rolled up in his two blankets, found the grassiest spot around and lay down. "Thank You for staying with me, anyway, Father," he said out loud looking up into the starry sky.

THE FAMILY JOINED DAVID OUTSIDE FOR BIBLE READING....

"I been in that creek so much, I'm near frozen. Would you mind keepin' me warm tonight? Thank You, God." A small crust of ice formed around the edges of any water left outside now, so David knew without special help he'd get real cold before morning.

By the time David turned over twice trying to get comfortable, a dark figure emerged from the house. It was Jake. "Thanks, Jake," David whispered. Jake said nothing but dropped his blankets a few feet from David and flopped to the ground.

David awakened to bright sun in the morning with no recollection of being cold.

He used a whole bar of soap in the creek every day for four days before Pa let him go inside.

"Want to go help me buy a plow?" Pa asked David a few days later. "I can't do much this fall, but I want to be ready early next spring."

Jake went, too, and they tried McMorris first.

"THANKS, JAKE," DAVID WHISPERED.

"Better try Fort Walla Walla," McMorris suggested.

Fort Walla Walla had several small plows they wanted to get rid of, so Pa and the boys picked one out and paid for it.

"You need some big horses to pull that?" the soldier asked.

Pa shook his head. "Thanks, but I have oxen." He shook his head again. "But they ain't here are they? Well, I reckon my boys'll bring the oxen to haul the thing home."

An hour later, Jake and David hooked the oxen to the plow, a small load for them, and headed home. David led the oxen, and Jake steered the plow. After going a little way, the oxen jerked, and bucked wildly until the nearest one knocked David to the ground. David looked back to see a long stick in Jake's hands. Jake pulled the stick back as if to poke the animals again.

JAKE PULLED THE STICK BACK TO POKE THE ANIMALS AGAIN.

"What do you think you're doing?" David screamed. "What's the matter with you? You trying to cripple them or what!"

Jake moved aside, laughing hard. "I just wondered what you'd do, Davy baby." David didn't see anything funny about it. He never saw anything funny about hurting an animal.

Jake slunk away, and David got the animals and the plow home alone.

David didn't tell Pa what had happened, but after they went to bed in the loft, he talked to Jake.

"Do you think Jesus would purposely hurt anyone— or even an animal?" he whispered.

Jake squirmed a little before he answered. "Naw. He wouldn't."

"Don't you want to belong to Jesus, Jake?"

"I do belong to Him."

"Well, do you love Him?"

"DON'T YOU WANT TO BELONG TO JESUS, JAKE?"

Jake hesitated. "Yeah. Do you, Davy baby?"

"Yes. A whole lot. But did you know the Bible says if we love Him, we'll obey His teaching? He commands us not to steal, Jake. If you love Him, you'll never steal again. You won't hurt people either, or even animals. You know you could have gotten me killed."

The boys fell asleep without saying anymore.

Two days later, Paul Reynolds, the Fort Walla Walla doctor, showed up again to check Pa. After examining his arms for some time, he looked happy. "How'd you like to get rid of those splints?" he asked.

Pa looked as if someone had handed him a grilled sunbeam on a plate of shredded sunshine. "I wouldn't mind that a bit. You gonna do it?"

Paul grinned. "I will if you promise to listen to me as well as you have up to now."

Pa still looked happy. "I guess I'll have to if I'm ever gonna get rid of these things. I'll do whatever

"HOW'D YOU LIKE TO GET RID OF THOSE SPLINTS?"

you tell me, Paul. Just take 'em off."

Paul took his time removing the splints. "You're doing better than I ever expected, Mr. Moreland. But you can't do anything for awhile. You won't even be able to use your arms."

Pa looked shocked. "Ain't they all right?"

Paul grinned. "They're great. Just fine. But you haven't moved them for six weeks. You'll have to teach them to move and work again—real slow like."

"Well, what're you waitin' for?"

David felt his heart beating hard as the doctor finished removing the splints, then the cloths—his and the doctor's shirts. David could hardly believe how Pa's arms looked. No wonder they looked so white, but why did they look only about half as big as they used to be? He asked the doctor.

Paul smiled kindly. "If you don't use your muscles, they shrivel up. They'll soon be all right, though." He

DAVID COULD HARDLY BELIEVE HOW PA'S ARMS LOOKED.

turned back to Pa. "The arms will hurt some. When they hurt, stop using them. Don't force them, or you could rebreak the bones. Now, let's see you bend your elbows."

Pa bent the right one just a little, then the left. He grimaced. "That hurt some. Guess I'll just have to make them work."

"Real easy," Paul said. He looked upward. "Thanks," he said softly. "You did a great job here, Lord. I guess You'll have to help him take it easy now." He took a step toward the cabin door. "Remember, I'm not far away. If you have trouble, just send one of the boys after me."

After he left, Pa sat on his log, bending first one arm then the other. David noticed sweat glistening on his upper lip. "He said not to force them, Pa. Better stop for now."

"How's bending my elbows gonna break a bone?"

"GUESS I'LL JUST HAVE TO MAKE THEM WORK."

Pa asked quietly. He kept right on, though David saw lots of pain in his eyes. "I'm gonna feed myself supper today," Pa said with a grim smile.

He did feed himself that night, too, though David thought his face looked whiter and stiffer than when he'd had the splints on.

Two days later, Annie and Mark came to talk to Pa. "Do we have to leave?" David asked.

Annie laughed. "Of course not. We want you here." David and Jake settled on the floor across the room.

Mark moved closer to Pa. "Annie and I've come to love each other, sir. I'd like to marry her, and we've have come for your blessing."

Jake gave a loud grunt and struggled to his feet. "I ain't listenin' to this stuff," he mumbled dashing out the door.

"I AIN'T LISTENIN' TO THIS STUFF."

"JAKE DOESN'T WANT YOU TO MARRY ANNIE."

CHAPTER 7

Mark stopped in the middle of a sentence. "What happened to him?" he asked.

"He doesn't want you to marry Annie," David said. "He liked Annie on The Trail. Didn't you notice when you came to work on the house, he left?"

Mark looked sad for a moment, then smiled. "He has good taste, but isn't he pretty young?"

"Don't worry about it," Pa said. He held his right hand out to Mark. "Shake that hand, boy, but easy-like. I'm proud to give you my blessing."

"Let's celebrate," Mama said. "I'll make a vanilla cake to eat with that leftover rice pudding."

An hour later, they ate the goodies Mama had fixed over the fire and planned the wedding. Mark and Annie wanted to be married right away, so the family decided to build a cabin for the happy couple.

The next morning Pa sent David to the store. "See if McMorris has any instructions for buildin' furniture. I could be studyin' how to do it while my arms get stronger."

While David saddled Thunder, Jake came galloping in from somewhere. Just as David started to mount Thunder, Jake rushed to the big horse's side and gave him a hard kick on the rear. The horse reared into the air, coming down beside David. David spoke softly to him and soon had him quiet enough to ride.

"Jake," David said as they headed toward The Street on their horses, "nothing I say to you sinks in, does it? The stuff you do isn't funny. It's plain mean. It makes God sad, too."

Jake hung his head. "I can't help it, Davy baby. Somethin' makes me do it. But I ain't stole nothin' lately."

McMorris had some rough instructions for furni-

"THE STUFF YOU DO ISN'T FUNNY."

ture, but he thought Baldwin at the trading post might have better ones. The boys left the horses and walked past Galbraith's Saloon. "This here's where they have church," Jake said. "I went there once, but three Injuns went, too. They stunk up the place so bad, I left."

Just as David started to reply, a dirty, skinny, middle-aged man came tearing out of the saloon and ran into David. "What ya think yer doin?" the man yelled, grabbing David and throwing him to the ground.

Almost before David hit the dirt, Jake put a fist into the man's sallow face. The man took two quick steps back. "Get outta here, you beggar," the man snarled at Jake. Then he started kicking David.

Jake applied a hard kick to the man's rear, sending him sprawling into the dusty street. Jake pulled back his foot again, but David interrupted.

"Don't, Jake. Leave him alone." Grabbing Jake's arm he dragged him across the street and on down to

"DON'T, JAKE. LEAVE HIM ALONE."

the traders.

Jake finally jerked away from David. "Why'd you go and do that?" he growled. "I 'bout had that runt squealin' like a pig."

David just kept going. The trading post had nothing, so they bought McMorris's instructions.

On the way home, David didn't say much. Neither did Jake. When they neared the cabin, Jake pranced his pony to Thunder's side. "Don't ya know why I beat that runt up? I did it fer you, Davy."

David nodded. "I know you did, Jake. Thanks. You're a good friend."

Pa smiled all over his face when David handed him the furniture plans. "I'll just look this over this afternoon," he said. "Why don't you boys go catch us some fish for supper?"

The boys hurried to the creek bank, dug some worms, saddled their horses, and raced to the river. A

"I DID IT FER YOU, DAVY."

half dozen boys of various sizes stood beside the river with fishing poles in their hands. As they moved to an empty spot along the stream, David noticed several baskets of fish, some really big.

"What kind of fish are you catching?" he asked a tall dark boy.

"Mostly trout," the boy eagerly explained. "That big one's a salmon. Ain't that some fish?"

"Yeah. I hope we catch something today. Last time, some Indian boys gave us part of theirs."

David and Jake prepared their poles and threw their lines into the water. And waited. And waited.

After awhile an Indian boy arrived, and soon another. Holding their lines in their hands, they tossed the baited hooks into the water. Almost right away, one of them caught a nice trout.

"What're we doing wrong?" David asked Jake.

"Whyn't you ask them Injuns?" Jake grunted.

"I HOPE WE CATCH SOMETHING TODAY."

David walked over to the Indians before wondering how he could talk to them. He pointed at the fish and showed he didn't have anything. Then he showed them his hook with a fishing worm on it and pointed into the water where their hooks were.

The Indian boy pulled his hook out of the water and showed David. The worm looked the same except the boy hadn't threaded the hook through it. He'd put the hook through the worm's body several times so the worm moved freely.

Ugh! David didn't like putting a hook through a live worm anyway, but he showed Jake how, and they both did it. Then they threw their hooks into the water. Still no fish.

After awhile, one of the Indians said something to the other and walked off. Pretty soon, the other followed, leaving their lines hooked to the basket of fish. Their lines swayed in the river current.

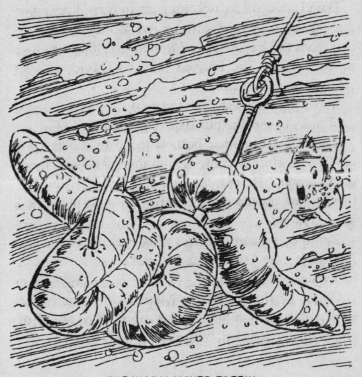

THE WORM MOVED FREELY.

David noticed Jake watching the Indians' lines more than his own. After awhile, a jerk nearly loosed the line from the basket. Jake jumped over there, pulled in a nice fish, and hurried back to David with it. "Here's one," he said.

"That isn't our fish," David said.

"Looks to me like our fish. I got it, don't I?"

They fished another hour with no luck. Jake got up. "There ain't no more fish in there," he said. "I'm goin' home." He marched calmly past the Indians' fish basket, picked it up, climbed onto his pony, and headed home.

David could hardly believe his eyes. Not only had Jake stolen the fish and basket, but six or seven boys had watched him do it.

When David got home, Mama, Katie, and Jake busily cleaned fish behind the cabin. "I'm proud of you boys," she called. "Supper is nearly ready."

DAVID COULD HARDLY BELIEVE HIS EYES.

David hardly knew what to do. How could he disappoint Mama? But he couldn't let Jake get away with stealing the fish. That would be bad for Jake and him, too.

"I'm sorry, Mama," he said, "but those aren't our fish. They belong to two Indian boys."

"Oh, sure," Jake said. "Whatever Davy baby does is all right. Whatever Jake does is wrong."

Mama turned back to Jake. "You said you caught them, Jake."

"I did catch one. Them redskins gave me the rest. They done caught so many, they don't even like 'em anymore."

Mama looked at David. He shook his head. "They didn't give them to Jake."

"He don't know everthin' goin' on in this world. Just go ahead 'n cook 'em."

Mama met David's eyes again. "I have to take his

"I DID CATCH ONE. THEM REDSKINS GAVE ME THE REST."

word for it," she whispered. "He needs someone to believe in him."

David didn't say anymore. He even ate one of the fish, though it bothered him some.

After supper, Pa called David and Jake to him. "I got some furniture figgered out while you were gone. I wrote down what I'll need to make it. Could you two go after some boards tomorrow?"

The next morning, David and Jake yoked the oxen and hooked them to the stripped-down wagon.

They arrived home late in the afternoon with all the boards Pa had asked for. The men at the mill had thrown in a few extra to show Pa how sorry they were about his accident.

Pa grinned when David told him. "I thank them," he said. "I won't be able to use the boards for awhile, but we'll have them here. In case it snows, I can still build the things when I get strong enough."

THEY ARRIVED HOME WITH THE BOARDS PA HAD ASKED FOR.

The next day, Jake wanted to go fishing again. David wasn't very sure he did, but Mama wanted some for supper. As the boys neared the river, David had a strong desire to turn around and go back. He couldn't do that, but why did they have to fish right here?

"Let's try a new fishing spot," he suggested.

Jake agreed, so they went a half-mile upstream. But when they reached the water, it didn't look so good, and it was a lot wider and shallower.

"Think a fish could grow in this water?" Jake asked.

David laughed. "We never caught anything down there, so we'll probably never know if there's fish here or not."

They prepared their gear, put their lines in the water, and sat under a tree to watch. Suddenly, Jake flipped his head back and looked in the tree. "I hear a 'possum up there."

"I HEAR A 'POSSUM UP THERE."

JAKE NEARED THE HOLE.

CHAPTER 8

David listened but didn't hear a thing. "What kind of sound does a 'possum make?"

Jake looked at him as if he were from another planet. "They hiss, stupid. Listen! He hears us. He's hissing louder'n I ever heard." He pointed to a hole in the tree about eight feet from the ground.

Throwing his fishing pole on the ground, he picked up a long stick. "I'm goin' after him," he said. "'Possums taste better 'n fish any old day."

David panicked for the little animal. "No, you aren't, Jake. It might have babies or—or anything. Don't you dare go up that tree."

Jake took his big stick and began reaching for one branch after another, quickly moving higher into the tree. As Jake neared the hole, David prayed. "Don't let him hurt the little animal, Father. It didn't do anything bad."

Just then Jake began to yell. "Ouch, help! Oh, it ain't a 'possum. Help, Davy. Quick!"

By the time David reached the tree, Jake hit the ground, too. His face, hands, neck, and even his hair—were all covered with bees!

Jake kept screaming and flinging his hands all over his body. "Ain't ya gonna help me, Davy? Ouch! Owww. They're killin' me!"

"Jump into the river, Jake! That'll get 'em off. Run!"

Jake looked at David, wild-eyed and still slapping at the bees. He didn't move toward the water. "Oh, I'm dyin'. Help! Davy, you know I can't swim."

"It isn't deep, Jake! You'll have to lie down on the rocks to get away from them. Go!"

Jake still didn't move, just slapped at bees and screamed in pain. David couldn't stand watching and listening any longer. He charged into Jake, bees and

"THEY'RE KILLIN' ME!"

all, and shoved him toward the river. A moment later, he gave the final push, and Jake splashed into the water. It came a little above his knees.

Some of the bees had discovered David, so he fell into the water to get away. The cold water felt comforting to the stings so he stayed in, ducking his head under part of the time. Soon the bees left.

They still surrounded Jake. "Get into the water!" David yelled. Jake swatted bees, screamed, and stood still. After awhile, David got cold and climbed out. He ran around trying to dry his clothes, until he felt so tired he'd drop, then climbed onto Thunder and went home.

"Where's the fish?" Katie asked.

In the excitement, David had forgotten what they'd gone for. "We didn't get any," he muttered running up the ladder to the loft to change into dry clothes.

"Where's Jake?" Mama wanted to know when

"GET INTO THE WATER!"

David came down.

"The last I saw, Jake stood in the river with bees swarming all over him."

Jake finally showed up just before dark, furious with David. "Ya don't care nothin' about me," he growled. "If'n you did, you'd never have gone off and left me like you did."

"I care enough about you to get all stung up," David said. "But the cold water helped my stings a lot."

Mama heard the boys snipping at each other. "Let me see your stings, Jake. Oh my, there are a lot all right. You wait right here while Davy gets some mud. I'll pack it on all of your stings. Do they still hurt a lot?"

Jake looked startled. "Mud? All over me? Naw, them stings don't hurt much at all anymore." He scrambled to his feet. "I better go. Pa has somethin' fer me to do."

"YA DON'T CARE NOTHIN' ABOUT ME."

After Jake left, the family laughed at his mishap. "We shouldn't laugh," Annie said. "But I'd rather it turn out this way than for it to have been a 'possum."

The next day, Pa started on the furniture. "I'll need you all day," he told David. "Paul's a right smart doctor. Leastwise, he knew my arms wouldn't be doin' much for awhile."

Jake came over but soon grew bored as the table Pa and David worked on wasn't changing very fast. "Think we could go fishin' this afternoon?" he asked as he left.

David looked at Pa. "I think you could," Pa said. "I'll be all played out by midafternoon."

David used Pa's plane to smooth the top of the table. Pa showed him where to put the screws to attach the legs to the table, then the braces. David began to feel some excitement over the table. It looked nicer than he'd expected.

DAVID USED PA'S PLANE TO SMOOTH THE TOP OF THE TABLE.

Katie hurried into the main room where Pa and David worked. "I had a good idea, Pa," she began hesitantly. "I was wondering if you and Davy could go back to that bee tree and get us some honey. Doesn't that sound good?"

For a fraction of a second, it sounded good to David, then he remembered his many stings—and Jake's even more stings. Besides that, Pa could never climb a tree with his arms. Jake would probably never go near a bee for the rest of his life. David would have to be the one to tangle with the bees. He looked at Pa, fearful of his answer.

But Pa shook his head. "Too late in the fall, Katie. If we take honey now, the bees might starve during the winter. We might take some in the spring, though."

David felt a big sigh of relief coming out of his mouth. Anything could happen by spring. The bees might even be gone.

"DOESN'T THAT SOUND GOOD?"

About midafternoon, Jake stopped and the boys went fishing again. "I don't know why we do this," David said. "We never have caught one."

"We will today," Jake said. "I got a special feelin'."

Jake led the way until they reached the spot where others fished. Today, three white boys and two Indians fished. David couldn't tell whether they were the ones from whom Jake had stolen the fish and basket.

David couldn't believe it when he felt a tug on his line and pulled in a twelve-inch beauty. A few minutes later, he got a little bigger one.

"Whatcha tryna do, make me look dumb?" Jake grumbled when David caught a fish about nine inches long.

David didn't want to get Jake mad. "Maybe we should trade poles," he suggested.

Jake didn't trade poles, but a half hour later when David caught his fourth fish, he threw his pole and

DAVID PULLED IN A TWELVE-INCH BEAUTY.

line into the water. He grabbed David's basket, marched over to a basket of fish no one guarded and took the three biggest fish. Jumping onto his horse, he kicked it hard. Before David or the other boys knew what had happened, Jake was a half mile away.

David didn't wait to see what the other boy thought, but grabbed Jake's pole from the water, hopped on Thunder, and took off after Jake.

"You seen Jake lately?" he asked Annie when Jake wasn't there.

"Not since this morning," Annie said. "Why don't you just be thankful he's gone for awhile?"

"'Cause he got the fish I caught. It's the first time I've caught any, and I wanted those fish bad."

The Moreland family didn't have fish for supper, but later Pa talked to David. "How'd you like to go get enough logs fer a cabin fer Annie and Mark?" he asked. "I'd give you and Jake each a nugget if you'd

DAVID DIDN'T WAIT TO SEE WHAT THE OTHER BOY THOUGHT. . . .

help through like you did last time."

David thought that sounded great. So the next day, when Pa got tired of working on the table, he went looking for Jake. He started to saddle Thunder but decided he'd rather walk this time.

He got about halfway to Jake's pa's tent when he met two white boys. "That's him!" one of them said. The boys turned around and jumped on David's back. He defended himself the best he could, but he couldn't handle two at a time. "How come you stole our fish?" one of the boys demanded as his fist smashed into David's ear.

"HOW COME YOU STOLE OUR FISH?"

JAKE'S FISTS AND FEET FLEW....

CHAPTER 9

David fell to the ground. Both boys dropped on him and started pounding. He knew for sure they'd give him a terrible beating now—for something he didn't do! But a whirlwind knocked them both off David. Jake! His fists and feet flew so fast, David couldn't keep track of them. But a moment later, one of the boys fell to the ground beside him, and the other sped across the dried grass as fast as he could go.

Jake drew back a foot to deliver a hard kick to the downed boy, but David grabbed the foot, causing Jake to fall hard on the ground. "He's down, Jake," David said. "Don't hurt him now."

"Whaddaya think yer doin'? Don't ya know it's me you knocked down?"

"I know, Jake, but you already whipped them. Why hurt him anymore?" The boy on the ground looked from David to Jake and back again. Then he crawled about ten feet, jumped to his feet, and ran the same direction his friend went.

David scrambled to his feet and headed toward his cabin. "Come on, Jake. I gotta talk to you."

Jake fell into step beside David, his scowl deepening. "Don't start tellin' me how rotten I am, Davy baby. I already know that. You don't like me anyway so why should I care? Your God don't like me neither, so why would I try to be a goody-goody like you?"

Jake's words hurt David worse than the other boys' fists had. "Let's walk on down to the river," he suggested, "where no one's fishing."

They settled in the sunshine on the bank. David didn't know what to say, but he had to say something. "What makes you think I don't like you, Jake?"

"Hoo, Davy baby. Ain't you ever heard yerself telling me how much better you are than me? It ain't hard to figger out."

"YOUR GOD DON'T LIKE ME NEITHER...."

David felt his stomach tighten. Did he really act that way? "I'm sorry, Jake. I don't mean to sound like that. Truth is, I like you a lot. I never had a brother, and you're almost my brother now."

Jake looked surprised. "Whyn't you say so? Well, Davy baby, maybe I can learn you how to be a little nicer to your friends. I mean, brother."

They started to get up, then David remembered Pa's offer. "Hey, I forgot something—brother. Pa said he'd give us each a nugget if we'll help build a cabin for Annie and Mark."

A smile half crossed Jake's face, then a big scowl replaced it. "You know I ain't buildin' them two a cabin. If I do anything for that coyote, it'll be puttin' out some poison meat."

David started home with Jake following. Somehow he had to get Jake to help. They needed him. "Think what we could do if we had those nuggets, Jake. Annie and Mark are getting married for sure. And someone's

"PA SAID HE'D GIVE US EACH A NUGGET IF WE'LL HELP...."

gonna earn money building their cabin. Why shouldn't it be us?"

Jake just grunted. David decided to let him think on it for a day or two.

The next day, Jake wandered to the Moreland cabin while David helped Pa finish up the table. He told Pa he'd be back and walked outside with Jake. "I figgered somethin' out," he told David. "Maybe you like me a little, but your God don't like me ever. At all."

David captured a tiny weed scurrying across the ground in the wind. "What makes you think that?" he asked quietly as he released the weed.

"'Cause everythin' I do is wrong. He don't never help me do nothin'. Or not to do nothin'."

David drew in a long breath. Jake had a big case of Nobody Likes Me. "Know how I know God loves me?"

Jake grunted and shrugged.

"I know 'cause the Bible tells me. Do you know

"...BUT YOUR GOD DON'T LIKE ME EVER. AT ALL."

how far heaven is above the earth, Jake? It's a long, long way. Farther than anything we can imagine. The Bible says He loves us that much. Did you know Jesus said His Father loves us as much as He loves Jesus?"

"That's you, Davy baby. I ain't as good as you. He don't love me none."

"No, Jake. Know when Jesus starts loving us?" Jake shook his head. "Well," David went on, "He loved us so much while we were sinners—that means when we were really bad—that He died for our sins."

Jake seemed deep in thought.

"Let's tell each other every day how much Jesus loves us, okay? We need to remember all the time."

"If He loves me like I am, why do I have to stop stealin'? And all the other stuff you keep yellin' about!"

Help me do this right, Father. And to be kind and gentle, David prayed silently. "Well, the Bible says if we love Him, we'll do as He asks. Know why He wants

"...IF WE LOVE HIM, WE'LL DO AS HE ASKS."

us to do that?"

"Guess I don't, Davy baby. Maybe He wants a bunch of little slaves."

David laughed. "He doesn't want slaves. The Bible tells us to treat others as we'd like to be treated. He does that so everyone can be happy. I didn't like it much when those boys beat me up. If you'd treated them nice, they wouldn't have done that. Get it, Jake?"

"Aw, I'm tired o' talkin' like this. Let's go home, Davy baby."

Jake decided to stay that night so they could start early to the mill. David had just fallen asleep when he heard loud voices downstairs. Somebody was yelling at Pa!

He jerked on his overalls and nearly fell getting down the ladder. Jake's pa was there—and mad about something.

"I just wanta know what's happenin'!" he yelled. "Those two men said my son stole fish from their boys.

JAKE'S PA WAS THERE—AND MAD ABOUT SOMETHING.

Whadda you know about this, Moreland?"

Pa seemed calm. "I guess you'd have to ask Jake about that, Mr. Case."

The man grabbed Pa by the arm and started jerking him around. David threw himself against the man, shoving him away. "Don't you touch my pa," he said quietly. "He's just getting over two broken arms. Want me to wake Jake up?"

Mr. Case stepped back and sort of crumbled. "Not tonight." He turned red eyes to Pa. "Sorry, Moreland. I forgot. I don't rightly know what to do. The man from the general store came one night 'n' tole me Jake stole a nugget and wanted me to give it back. I ain't got that kind of money.

"Another time a man came 'n' said my boy threw a bucket of water from the creek on his wife and daughter. He wanted me to tan Jake's hide. I ain't even sure I'm man enough to do that anymore. What should I do, Mr. Moreland?"

"DON'T YOU TOUCH MY PA."

Pa shifted his feet some but didn't say anything.

"I'm trying to help him, Mr. Case," David said quietly. "I'm teaching him about God's love. Could you give me a little more time?"

The man's head dropped. When he looked up, his eyes looked like a scared animal. "Don't got no choice, I reckon. Things woulda bin different if my wife had lived." He walked to the door. "Thanks fer listenin'. And fer whatever you can do fer my boy." He stepped through the door into the dark night.

The next morning, Jake and David ate an early breakfast, put the lunch Mama made for them into the wagon, and headed into the Blue Mountains for logs.

They returned in time for supper, tired but jubilant with a day's work well done.

The following Sunday, the preacher from the saloon came and married Annie and Mark. The family celebrated afterwards with a big roast David brought from the meat market.

"THINGS WOULDA BIN DIFFERENT IF MY WIFE HAD LIVED."

After the celebration ended, Annie and Mark went to Martin's boardinghouse where Mark lived. They had to get married before they built the cabin so they could get their donation land claim to build it on. They chose a piece of land on the same creek as the Moreland place, but just below.

David and Jake made several more trips to the mill for logs and boards. Then they worked on the cabin with Mark, Annie, and Katie. Pa still couldn't use his arms much, so he did his helping from a log. Ma made meals.

Jake made sure he never worked with Mark, but made only a few unpleasant remarks.

The happy group finished the cabin in two weeks, and the newlyweds moved in.

Pa gave Jake and David their nuggets. David put his in the bottom of his clothes pile. He never saw Jake's again.

Thanksgiving came with much colder weather and

PA GAVE JAKE AND DAVID THEIR NUGGETS.

a little rain. Mama cooked a big meal for the entire family. They invited Jake and his pa, but only Jake came. They had a meat roast, mashed potatoes and gravy, baked squash, dried peas, spiced carrots, mince meat, and pumpkin pies. Mama cooked everything over the fireplace as she still didn't have a cook stove.

The weather didn't cool much in December, so Jake and David made two more trips to the mill after boards for furniture for both cabins.

Then Pa sent them after three more loads of logs to build a barn. David cut two Christmas trees and threw them on top of the last load.

"May we string popcorn for the tree?" Katie asked that evening.

DAVID CUT TWO CHRISTMAS TREES.

...THEY FINISHED BUILDING THE BARN.

CHAPTER 10

Soon, white strings of popped corn made the tree festive. Mama found some red material which they tied around walnuts and hung them on branches between the strings of popcorn. Katie pronounced the tree perfect.

Back home in Independence everyone always hoped for a white Christmas. But they hardly ever had one. The Morelands didn't have a white Christmas in their new home in Walla Walla Valley, either.

Soon after Christmas, they finished building the barn. Everyone got bored sitting inside through the winter, but Pa grew strong and healthy.

Jake spent about half his time with the Morelands and continued to plague the family with his mean tricks. David kept telling him how much Jesus loved him. He needed to keep reminding himself, too. It helped him be kind to Jake.

Spring came early in 1860. February drizzle gave way to two, warm, sunny weeks, and the March sunshine tempted the new settlers outside to start the spring plowing.

Pa took David out with him in mid-March, and the two began plowing the vast fields. David walked behind the single bottom plow, watching its big point dig into the earth, turning over a strip about a foot wide.

Before a week passed, Pa realized what a huge job they'd laid out for themselves. They rode over to Fort Walla Walla and bought another plow, two disks, and two large work horses.

David used the horses, and as soon as he learned how to plow with them, he took a morning and worked up a big vegetable garden near the cabin for Mama and Katie to plant.

DAVID WALKED BEHIND THE SINGLE BOTTOM PLOW.

Following the horses, David loved hearing the songs of the newly returned meadowlarks. And watching them, the robins and killdeers following the plow, catching the worms and insects he turned up. Rabbits scampered here and there, and once or twice each day, he caught sight of a graceful deer bounding across the prairie.

After a month of plowing all day, they used the disks over the ground to smooth out the clods so they could plant the barrels of precious alfalfa seed they'd brought from Missouri. The men at Fort Walla Walla had agreed to buy all the hay they could produce, so Pa had high plans of making lots of money this fall. Alfalfa didn't have to be replanted each year, so next year they'd be able to cut it more than once.

David cared for the horses and Pa the oxen. David loved the animals and didn't mind spending time currying, feeding, and watering them as well as cleaning

ROBINS AND KILLDEERS FOLLOWED THE PLOW.

the small barn.

Every family member looked forward to the Sabbath day to rest the animals and themselves. Pa usually preached a little sermon, and the family sang many songs from the old hymnal Mama had tucked into a trunk. Each member of the family always prayed and told the others how they'd seen God in their lives that week.

One day in May when the vegetable gardens were planted and the crops nearly in, Jake ate dinner with the Morelands, which wasn't unusual. "Ain't you never goin' to be able to go fishin' agin?" he fussed. "Them fish oughta be bitin' good by now."

Pa smiled at his son, grown tall and strong from his hard work, and already brown from the spring sun. "Why don't you quit a bit early tonight and see what you can catch. Fresh fish sounds good to me."

Later, Jake fussed while David cared for his horses.

"FRESH FISH SOUNDS GOOD TO ME."

David ignored Jake and did everything for the faithful animals they needed. They worked hard and deserved it.

They shared the fishing hole with several white boys, a few girls, and three Indian boys about their age. The white young people all called to each other and laughed together. The Indians remained quiet.

"Are you catching anything?" David asked.

"Not much," the boy answered. "Them fish ain't much awake for spring yet."

That seemed to be the story with all the whites, but the Indians quietly brought in one fish after another.

David caught two small fish and Jake one, in the two hours they fished. David gave Jake his fish and hurried into the house to eat and go to bed. He'd worked about eleven hours that day, a couple fewer than usual.

Two weeks later, Pa and David finished seeding

"THEM FISH AIN'T MUCH AWAKE FOR SPRING YET."

the last acre of alfalfa and returned the two borrowed seeders to Fort Walla Walla. Pa acted jubilant. "I dunno what we'll do until harvest time, but I'll bet it'll be somethin'."

"Maybe you'll go fishin' with us, Pa," David suggested.

"I might at that, son. Well, I 'spect we'll have more money 'n we ever dreamed about from that new kind of hay. In the meantime, I guess I got a lot more furniture to make fer your ma."

The next day, David and Jake rode to town to look for a small saw for Pa, to make dainty cuts.

"Sounds to me like The Tin Shop would be most like to have a special-type saw," Jake said.

So the boys stopped there first. The man there said he didn't have one and neither would McMorris. But David decided he'd check anyway. Pa really needed that saw.

PA REALLY NEEDED THAT SAW.

McMorris and David went into the back and sorted through a big pile of equipment until David spotted a saw that might work. McMorris added it to the Moreland bill, and David discovered Jake had gone without him again. Oh well. He was getting used to Jake's impatience by now.

McMorris rode up just before dark that night. "That other kid here?" he bellowed when David stepped out the cabin door.

"Not right now." David called back. "Could I help you?"

"I doubt you want to be responsible for him!" He turned his horse and took off east.

"What did McMorris want?" Pa asked when David came back in.

"I dunno, Pa. I bet Jake took something again."

Jake didn't show up for a few days.

Pa got up one morning seeming extra chipper. After breakfast, he cornered David. "How'd you like to

"THAT OTHER KID HERE?"

get some honey, Dave?"

The horror of a million stings came back to David in a hurry. "I'm not sure, Pa. How'd we keep from getting stung up?"

"Well, bee stings don't hurt much do they?"

"They hurt me. Really bad."

Pa thought a bit. "Maybe if we went at night, they'd be mostly asleep. I'll get the honey, Dave. All you have to do is go with me. Maybe I'll hand you the bucket of honey if I get too much."

About the time Mama and Katie went to bed that night, Pa and David headed for the bee tree. They decided not to tell the women, so they'd be surprised.

When they reached the tree, David pointed to the hole. He could barely see it by the light of the half moon.

"Well, that's not very high," Pa said. "I'll just take the bucket and get right on up there." A few moments later, he stood on a limb, looking into the hole. "I don't

PA STOOD ON A LIMB, LOOKING INTO THE HOLE.

hear anything," he whispered. "Guess they're asleep all right."

He reached his arm into the hole, jerked it back and began yelling. "Ouch, ooow, oohhhh. That's not bees in there, Davy. It's some kind of animal, and it bit my finger clean off."

"...IT BIT MY FINGER CLEAN OFF."

"NAW. A BEAR REALLY WOULD HAVE BITTEN MY FINGER OFF."

CHAPTER 11

Pa came tumbling down from the tree and held his hand out to David. Unable to see in the dark, David felt the bloody hand, then sighed with relief. The animal had hurt Pa for sure, but it hadn't bitten his finger off.

When they got home, Mama got out of bed and soaked the finger in epsom salts. "Serves you right for trying to take something from the bees," she scolded, her eyes twinkling.

"Think that could have been a bear, Pa?" David asked.

Pa shook his head. "Naw. A bear really would have bitten my finger off. Anyways, that hole wasn't near big enough fer a bear." He thought a moment and laughed. "Probably a 'possum hole, just like Jake said."

"Might've been, Pa, but I guarantee bees came out of that hole last fall and like to stung us to death."

Pa healed up in a couple of days then found plenty to do—for him and David, too.

The next time Jake came over, David told him about Pa getting bit at the bee tree.

"Wanna go see what that animal is?" Jake asked.

David held his hands out as if warding off an animal. "Not for anything, Jake. First, it was a 'possum, then bees. Now we don't know what it was, and I'm afraid to find out. Want to go fishing?"

The cloudy day discouraged fishing, so they saw only two white boys and two Indians, fishing in the river, about thirty feet apart.

They played around with the white boys and mostly ignored the Indians, but David couldn't help noticing a huge fish one of the Indian boys dragged from the water.

His mouth dropped open. "What's that?" he asked,

THE INDIAN BOYS DRAGGED A HUGE FISH FROM THE WATER.

pointing.

"Looks like a salmon," one of the boys said. "I seen one bigger'n that a long time ago." They all watched the Indian remove the hook and drop the fish on the ground beside the basket which was much too small to hold the fish.

Soon, the boys forgot the fish and took up their own fishing and playing again.

"I just remembered Pa wants me to do somethin' fer him this afternoon," Jake said, pulling in his line. A few minutes later, David waved to him as he rode away on his spotted pony.

About five minutes later, the Indian boys returned from somewhere and sat down by the river again, holding their lines in their hands. A few minutes later, David heard a distressed cry and looked to see the Indians searching all around their fish basket. Their big fish had disappeared!

THEIR BIG FISH HAD DISAPPEARED!

After looking for a few more minutes, one of the Indian boys ran straight to David. He leaned over him and began yelling at him. David couldn't understand a word, but he knew the boy was mad.

The Indian jerked him to his feet, then made motions to show the big fish.

Now he knew! The Indian thought he'd taken his fish. He shook his head no and showed the Indian his basket with two small fish. Then he tipped his hands outward in an empty position.

The Indian motioned toward Thunder, then held up two fingers and motioned a quick out-of-here motion.

The Indian thought Jake took the fish. And suddenly, David did, too. But what could he do? He just shook his head. And showed empty hands again. Before he knew what had happened, the Indian jumped onto him, kicking and pounding so fast David couldn't even think.

THE INDIAN JERKED HIM TO HIS FEET. . . .

Finally, he managed to grab the other boy's hands and threw him to the ground. As David held the Indian boy down, the other one jumped on his back and threw him to the ground.

Between the two, they beat David until he quit trying to get up. When David lay completely still, they walked off, gathered up their things, and left the river.

David looked around, feeling his eyes swelling shut. He could still see the white boys, pale-looking, and saying nothing. Why hadn't they helped him as the Indian had helped his friend? He knew why! They thought he and Jake planned stealing the fish together.

Everyone thought he was a thief—just like Jake!

That hurt more than the beating had. He could never steal anything, and he didn't want anyone thinking he would.

Not brave enough to face the boys, he lay there unmoving until the last one had left. Then he struggled

THEY BEAT DAVID UNTIL HE QUIT TRYING TO GET UP.

onto Thunder's back and rode home.

Mama hurried out to get David's fish. "What?" she asked in good humor. "When you were so late, I expected you to have a dozen. Oh well, we'll eat side meat."

After David put Thunder away and went inside for supper, everyone noticed his bruises and scrapes. He told them what had happened. "I'm sure Jake took that great fish, Pa. I wish he could have taken his own beating."

Jake didn't come around for more than a week. David didn't ever want to see him again. He and Pa pulled weeds from the vegetable garden and carried water to some of the plants.

"Jake's never going to be a Christian, is he, Pa?" David asked while they worked.

Pa straightened up, rubbed the middle of his back, and looked David in the eye. "We can't never say that,

"JAKE'S NEVER GOING TO BE A CHRISTIAN, IS HE, PA?"

son. God didn't give up on us, and we're never to give up on anybody. Jake may be sorry already."

David grinned. "That doesn't help my beating much. And even worse, those white boys think I'm just like Jake."

Pa grinned back at him. "Don't you worry about that, son. You just live for God, and one of these days, those boys will know what you are."

One evening, Jake came back looking far from cocky. In fact, he looked as if he hadn't a friend in the entire world.

He held out a note to David. Reluctantly, David took it and read:

Fer Jake:
Since you like them people who think ther better 'n' us, why don't you jest go liv with 'em? All yer doin' is ruinin' my gud

HE LOOKED AS IF HE HADN'T A FRIEND IN THE ENTIRE WORLD.

name. Those Indians came agin. Said they're gonna git our scalps. I'm gettin' out. Headin' fer the Californy gold mines. Don't wait fer me 'cause I ain't comin' back. Never.

Pa

David met Jake's sad eyes. Jake nodded. "Yep, he done left. Ain't been back fer two days."

David didn't know what to do. "I better get Pa," he finally said. "Come on in." He ran into the house, and Jake followed. Pa sat at the new table writing something. David held out the note. "Look, Pa. See what Jake brought over."

Pa read the paper and handed it to Mama who sat on the other side of the table embroidering. When Ma finished, she laid her pillow case down, hurried to Jake and pulled him to her. "What will you do, you poor boy?"

"WHAT WILL YOU DO, YOU POOR BOY?"

Jake squirmed away. "Stay at the tent I guess. Maybe someone'll hire me so I can buy food."

Pa didn't say a word, and suddenly, David felt fearful that Ma and Pa would take him in. And he didn't want Jake around all the time. He didn't want Jake around any of the time.

Jake reached for the note, and Mama put it into his hand. "Guess I'll be goin' now," he said. "See ya, Davy baby."

"Well, what are we going to do about that?" Mama asked. "We can't let the poor boy starve, can we?"

"Let's not rush into anything," Pa said. "Let's just think about it awhile. I want to help Jake, but we gotta think of our own first." In a little while, everyone went to bed.

David lay in the loft on his mat thinking. They didn't even ask what he thought. Come to think of it, he didn't know what he thought, now that Jake didn't have a pa.

"GUESS I'LL BE GOIN' NOW. SEE YA, DAVY BABY."

The next day, Jake came about dinner time and Mama asked him to eat with them. David noticed that he ate a lot more than usual. Maybe he didn't have enough to eat in the tent.

He stayed and helped David feed and water the animals, then for supper. Mama had cooked a big stew. Jake ate three big bowls and three fat slices of homemade bread with butter.

Then he stayed through Bible reading and prayer and left.

He kept up the same schedule for a week. Not once did he do something mean to David or anyone else in the family. David mentioned it to Mama and Pa.

"He ain't so dumb," Pa said. "He ain't going to bite the hand that feeds him."

"Or maybe he's really trying to change his life around," Mama said.

David decided to talk to Jake the next day, so when

"HE AIN'T GOING TO BITE THE HAND THAT FEEDS HIM."

they finished caring for the animals they sat in the hay. "Did you know the Indians beat me up real bad when you stole their big fish?" he asked.

Jake looked shocked. "Hoo! I din't mean fer that to happen."

"I know, Jake, but you have to remember if we love God, we'll do as He asks us."

Jake nodded. "I know, Davy. I ain't stolen nothing since that fish. I ain't goin' to steal nothin' ever again, neither. I promise."

David had an idea. "Will you follow me in making a promise to God?"

Jake nodded. "I'll do anythin' you want."

David shook his head. "It's not what I want," he said. "It's what God wants. And what's best for you." He took both of Jake's hands in his. "Okay, here we go, Jake. Dear Father in heaven." Jake repeated it. "I realize how much You love me." Jake repeated it too.

"THE INDIANS BEAT ME UP REAL BAD...."

"I know You love me more than I can ever understand." Jake said the words, still holding David's hands. "I want to surrender my whole life to You." Jake said the words. "Forgive my sins. I love You, and with Your help, will do whatever You ask." Jake bowed his head and said the words. "I'll praise Your name forever and ever." Some tears ran down Jake's cheeks as he repeated the words.

David jumped up from the hay and awkwardly hugged Jake while Jake acted embarrassed. "That's all, Jake. You belong to Jesus now just like me. He'll guide your every step and even your thoughts, if you'll let Him."

Jake edged toward the barn door. "Thanks, Davy baby," he mumbled before taking off across the prairie.

That night, Pa and Mama talked to Katie and David. "What do you two think should happen to Jake?" Pa asked.

SOME TEARS RAN DOWN JAKE'S CHEEKS
AS HE REPEATED THE WORDS.

"I like him. I think we should adopt him," Katie said quickly.

Mama nodded. "And you, Dave? What do you think?"

"It's all right with me. After we did the chores today, he gave his heart to God. I don't think he'll give anyone any more trouble."

Pa smiled and reached for Ma's hand. "I guess we have our job cut out for us. God's been with us every step gettin' the land tamed. That alfalfa's goin' to give us plenty of money. Our God ain't gonna do less if we take in a poor homeless boy to tame. Why don't you go get him, Davy, and tell him he has a home now."

"I LIKE HIM. I THINK WE SHOULD ADOPT HIM."

WAGONS
WEST

AT A CHRISTIAN BOOKSTORE NEAR YOU

POCAHONTAS

Awesome

Books for Kids!

Young Reader's Christian Library
Action, Adventure, and Fun Reading!

Abraham Lincoln	Paul
At the Back of the North Wind	Peter
Ben-Hur	Pilgrim's Progress, The
Christopher Columbus	Pocahontas
Corrie ten Boom	Pollyanna
David Livingstone	Prudence of Plymouth Planation
Elijah	Robinson Crusoe
Heidi	Roger Williams
Hudson Taylor	Ruth
In His Steps	Samuel Morris
Jesus	Swiss Family Robinson, The
Joseph	Taming the Land
Lydia	Thunder in the Valley
Miriam	Wagons West